Published by Octobre Press

606 Azalea Lane, Vero Beach, Florida 32963

Illustrations by Virginia Best

Editorial Development by Laura Ross

Art Editing by Cynthia Bardes

Assistant Art Editing by Amanda Robinson

Assistant Art Editing by David

PRINTED IN THE UNITED STATES

This book was typeset in Berkeley.

ISBN 978-0-692-98457-4

Please visit the website for more information

www.PansythePoodle.com

Pansy in Africa
The Mystery of the Missing Lion Cub

written by Cynthia Bardes   illustrations by Virginia Best

Pansy at the Palace
A Beverly Hills Mystery
written by Cynthia Bardes illustrations by Kim Weissenborn

Pansy in Paris
A Mystery at the Museum
written by Cynthia Bardes illustrations by Virginia Best

Pansy in Venice
The Mystery of the Missing Parrot
written by Cynthia Bardes illustrations by Virginia

Pansy toy dog

Pansy in New York
The Mystery of the Missing Monkey
written by Cynthia Bardes illustrations by Virginia Best

Pansy in London
The Mystery of the Missing Puppy
written by Cynthia Bardes illustrations by Virginia Best

Titles available in the Pansy the Poodle Mystery Series

for Avery, Aubrey, Cindy, and David

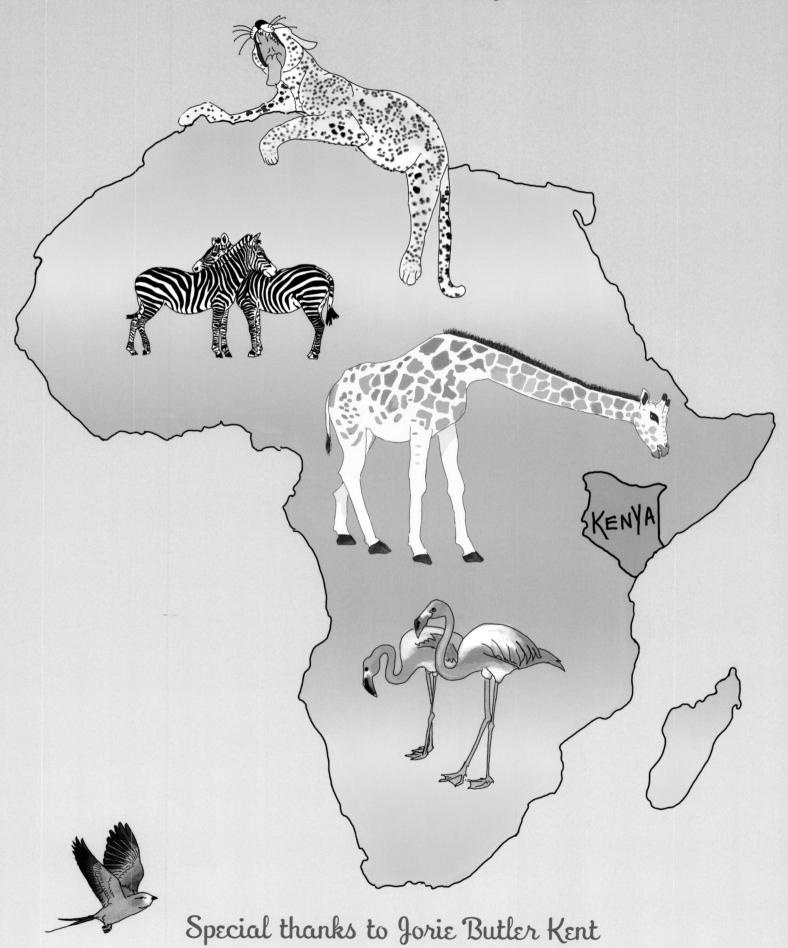

KENYA

Special thanks to Jorie Butler Kent

My name is Pansy. I am a toy poodle and a world-famous detective, and I live with my best friend Avery. Mama and Daddy brought us to Africa to go on a safari. Avery told me that *safari* means a trip to see animals where they live!

"*Karibu!* That means welcome," said a man. "I am your guide, Gregory. I will take you to our camp. Tomorrow we will go on safari."

"Yip, yip," I said. *Let's get going!*

"Look, Pansy, up in that tree!" said Avery. "I think that's a leopard!"

"That is called a sausage tree," said Gregory.

"Woof!" I said. The leopard yawned and showed his pointy teeth. Then we saw some more big cats, right in the road.

"Those are lions," said Avery. "The one with the big hair is the daddy. I wonder why they are crying? How sad."

"The lions are crying because one of their cubs is missing," said Gregory. "Her name is Zuri."

"Pansy is a detective," said Avery. "Maybe she can help you find Zuri!"

That night, we slept in a big tent that had a zipper for a door.
All night long, I could hear grunts and howls and snorts and growls.

"Awhoooo," I yowled, trying to join in.

"Go to sleep, Pansy," said Avery. "We have a big day tomorrow—and a mystery to solve."

Early the next morning, Gregory came to wake us.

"*Jambo*," he said. "That means *hello*. Are you ready to look for animals?"

"*Jambo*," said a young man dressed in a red cloth and beads. "My name is Hodari and I am from the Maasai tribe."

"Woof, woof," I said. *You are very tall!*

"Hello, Hodari, I am Avery and this is Pansy the poodle detective."

"Gregory, we want to find Zuri," said Avery, "but first we'll need some clues."

"Hmmm," said Gregory. "Zuri loves to visit our camp and lie under the gardenia bushes. She always smells like gardenias. She likes to leap and dance and make us laugh."

"Those are very good clues," said Avery.

"Yip, yip," I said. I was in a hurry to look for the missing lion cub.

"I want to help, too," said Hodari. "I have seen Zuri many times. The other lion cubs make fun of Zuri because she is different and has a crooked paw. She cannot run and hunt with them and likes to search for gardenias instead."

"Woof, woof!" I ran over to sniff a gardenia bush so I could remember the smell. *No wonder Zuri likes gardenias,* I thought. *Mmmmmm!*

"Let's start looking right away," said Hodari.

I started down a dirt path, sniffing all the way. Avery and Hodari followed me.
Then I saw it: a crooked paw print!

We followed the paw prints all the way to a lake full of big pink birds whose legs were like sticks.

"Those are flamingos," said Hodari. "They are pink, because they eat shrimp."

I kept following Zuri's crooked paw prints right to a gardenia bush. *Sniff, sniff—yum!*

"Look at the giraffes!" said Avery.

Hodari said, "They are so tall that they eat the leaves right off the Acacia trees, and make them look like umbrellas. We call them 'Africa's gardeners.'"

"Woof, woof," I said, looking at their long, long necks. *Let's keep going!*

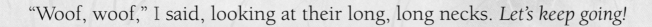

I followed Zuri's paw prints to a clearing and saw eyes and ears sticking out of the water.

"Hippopotamuses stay under water most of the time," said Hodari. "In this way they do not get sun burned. See how they eat the water lettuce? It is their favorite."

"Ooh, there's a hippo over there, too!" said Avery. "And look at the zebras! They look like they are wearing striped pajamas!"

We kept following the paw prints until we came
to a family of elephants eating plants and leaves and grass.

Hodari told me the grass is called *elephant grass.*

Even the baby is very big, I thought. *I am glad elephants eat plants!*

As we hurried through the grass, something whizzed by us
in a big flurry of spots and dots.

"Cheetahs!" said Hodari. "They are the fastest cats of all."

We continued through grass so tall that it covered me up.
I couldn't find any more paw prints, but I could smell . . . gardenias!
"Arf, arf!" *This way!*

As we came out of the grass, I saw a man with a funny cap holding a movie camera.

We looked to see what he was filming and there was Zuri the lion cub, leaping in the air, prancing and dancing like a ballerina.

"Yip, yip, yip!" I said.

"CUT!" yelled the man, lowering his camera and frowning at me.

"Grrrrr," I said.

Zuri stopped dancing and began licking her paw.

"Who are you?" Hodari asked the man.

"And why have you taken Zuri away from her family?" asked Avery.

"I am Phillip and I make movies about animals," said the man. "I found Zuri lying under a gardenia bush. When she saw me she jumped up and began to twirl and whirl and make me laugh and clap. I wanted to make a movie about the dancing lion cub! Zuri is very special."

Zuri rubbed against Phillip's legs and purred like a kitten.
I could see that she liked Phillip.

"You should not have taken Zuri!" said Hodari.

"Her family is very worried," said Avery. "We need to take her back right away!"

"Woof, woof, woof," I said, thinking about the crying lions.

Everyone followed me back to camp.
"Awhooo," I howled.

"Squeee," said Zuri, which was as much of a roar as she could make.

Soon, Zuri's mama and daddy came out of the trees, along with Zuri's twin brother, Kito.

They gave Zuri big lion hugs.

Gregory gave Zuri a gardenia. "Phillip," he said, "Africa is a place where the animals are free. You must never take an animal from its mama and daddy."

"I am very sorry," said Phillip, taking off his cap. "What can I do to make everyone happy?"

Squawkity
Squawk

Squeakity
Squeee

"I have an idea," said Avery. "Let's show the movie about Zuri
to all of the animals. Then they will see how special she is."

"What a wonderful idea!" said Hodari. "I will ask the horned-beak bird to invite all of the
animals to the movie."

"Squawkity-squawk! Squeakity-squeeee!" the bird cried. "*Come to the show!*"

Soon, many different animals gathered to see the movie. Even a shy baby rhinoceros stood quietly, watching Zuri leap and dance on the screen.

When the movie was over, the animals cheered and so did Avery and I.

"Dance for us! Please, dance for us, Zuri!" the other animals shouted. "We are sorry that
we were mean to you. We want to be friends!"

"Pansy," said Gregory, "thank you for finding Zuri and bringing her back to her family. Now, I want to do something for you and take you on a special safari tomorrow."

"I can make a movie for you to take back home," said Phillip.

Avery thanked Phillip and then spoke to the other lion cubs and animals.

"You must never make fun of anyone, and always treat others as you want to be treated. Remember it is our differences that make us special!"

"Yip, yip, YIPPEEE," I said, and began to twirl and dance. Zuri and Avery joined me. We were so happy to know that Zuri had friends now, who like her just the way she is.

"This has been an amazing trip, Pansy!" said Avery, hugging me tight. "Think of all the animals we've seen!"

"Yes it was amazing," I thought. *I love Africa and I love you.*
And I gave my best friend a kiss.

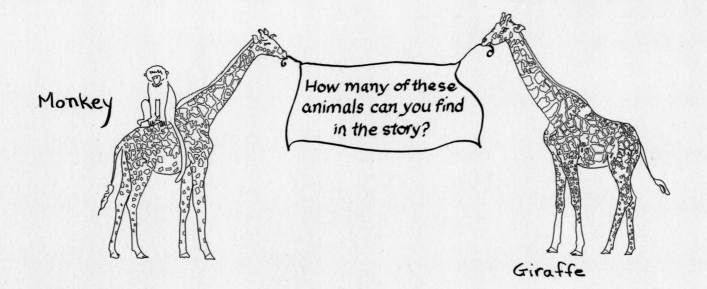

Monkey

How many of these animals can you find in the story?

Giraffe

Rhinoceros

Wildebeest

Elephant

Cheetah

Helmeted Guinea Fowl